Hush Little Polar Bear

ISBN 978-0-545-82028-8

Published by Scholastic Inc., 557 Broadway, New York, NY 10012,
by arrangement with Roaring Brook Press, a division of
Holtzbrinck Publishing Holdings Limited Partnership.
SCHOLASTIC and associated logos are trademarks and/or
registered trademarks of Scholastic Inc.

12 11 10 9 8 7 6 5 4 3 2 1   15 16 17 18 19 20/0

Printed in the U.S.A.   40

First Scholastic printing, January 2015

Hush Little Polar Bear

JEFF MACK

SCHOLASTIC INC.

Hush little polar bear.
Sleep in the snow,
and dream of the places
where sleeping bears go.

Sail the high seas on the back of a whale.

Land on a beach,
and then follow a trail.

Wade through a marsh
where the tall grasses grow,

where butterflies flutter
and warm breezes blow.

Bounce through a pasture
where cows come to graze.

Creep through a cave
with an underground maze.

Swim through a waterfall.
Splash in a stream.
Paddle past rainbows
that glisten and gleam.

Swing through the trees from a dangling vine.

Forge through a desert where stars shimmer and shine.

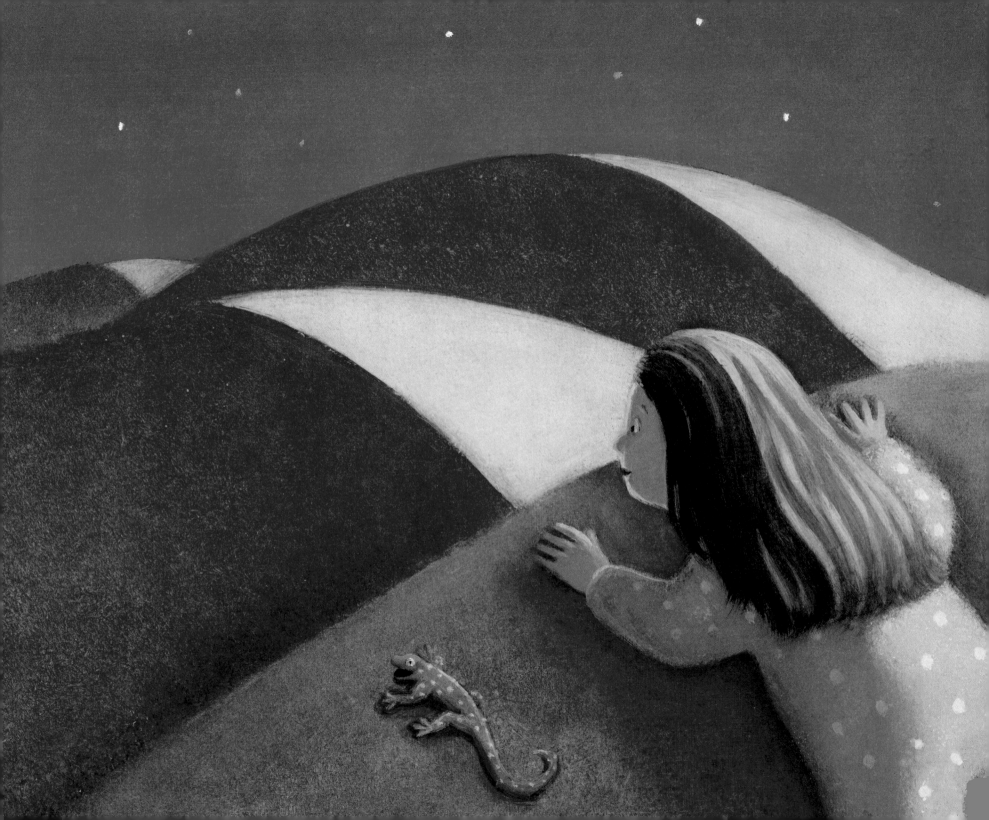

Climb a tall mountain where
billy goats play,
where breezes grow cooler
and clouds fade away.

Leap from the peak

and then float through the sky.

Soar as the hawks and the eagles fly by.

Dive through the clouds
to a town far below
with the lights from the streetlamps
and houses aglow.

Drift through my window.
Crawl into bed.
Curl up beside me
and rest your sweet head.

Pretend that you're sleeping
and dreaming like me.

Then look right beside you,
and that's where I'll be.